For Elliot, Harvey, and Rosie

The Struggle Bus is published by
Kind World Publishing
PO Box 22356
Eagan, Minnesota 55122
www.kindworldpublishing.com

Text and illustrations copyright © 2022 by Julie Koon
Cover illustrations copyright © 2022 by Julie Koon
Cover design by Tim Palin Creative
Book design by Katherine Liestman

Published in 2022 by Kind World Publishing.

Printed in the United States of America.

ISBN 978-1-63894-001-2 (hardcover)
ISBN 978-1-63894-008-1 (ebook)

Library of Congress Cataloging-in-Publication Data is available on the Library of Congress website.
Library of Congress Control Number: 2021922900

THE STRUGGLE BUS

Story and pictures by
Julie Koon

Kind
World
PUBLISHING
Eagan, Minnesota

Sometimes things are really tough.
It's just too hard. You've had enough.

You try and try

but you lose hope.

You'll never get it.
No way,
nope.

Grumble, rumble, bump, and roar,

the struggle bus is at your door.

You climb aboard
and take a seat,
hang your head,
accept defeat.

It may feel like
it's just you,
but all of us have
been there too.

Grumble, rumble, bump, and blow,

the struggle bus begins to go.

You can cry,

or you can shout,

kick and scream

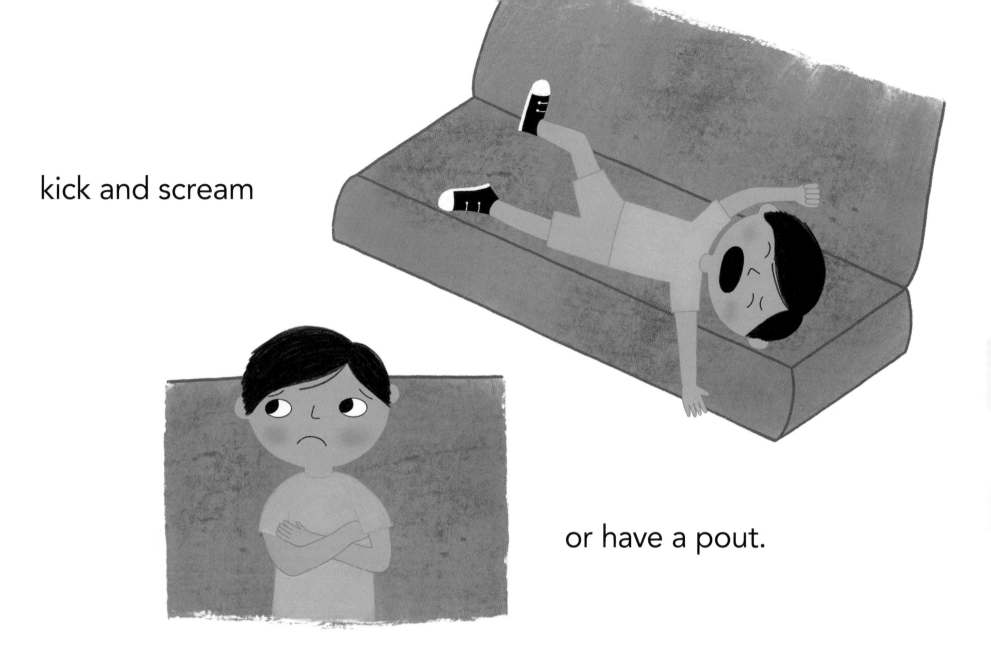

or have a pout.

Feel your feelings for a bit.
Just keep moving—
don't you quit!

Grumble, rumble, bump, and yawn,

Fog creeps in and rain comes down.

Make a left,

no, turn around.

LOST →

← MORE LOST

Trudging on,
you're filled with dread,
and things look
even worse ahead.

Grumble, rumble, bump, and frown,

oh no, the struggle bus breaks down.

When the tools you have fall short,
it's ok to get support.

Friends who've gone through this before
can give you wings and help you . . .

SOAR!

Grumble, rumble, bump, and fly,

the struggle bus is soaring high.

Above the clouds you have great views,
but you're not sure which way to choose.

You search and circle with concern,

and you're more lost

with every turn.

Grumble, rumble,
bump, and groove,

the struggle bus
is on the move.

As the wheels turn
round and round,
your brain does too,
your path is found.

Faster now,
the way is clear.
You can do it,
persevere!

Grumble, rumble, bump, and bop,
the struggle bus comes to a stop.

You clambered, conquered, made it through.
And now you're braver, tougher too.

No matter what the future brings,
you're strong enough to do hard things.

Keep rolling on.

What is one thing that was hard for you today?

Perseverance means never giving up and continuing to try until you achieve your goal. But how does it work?

Your brain has cells called neurons that are like tiny roads. These roads connect to each other when you learn new things. Each time you practice something, the road gets bigger and bigger until it becomes like a highway. Then the task is easy for you.

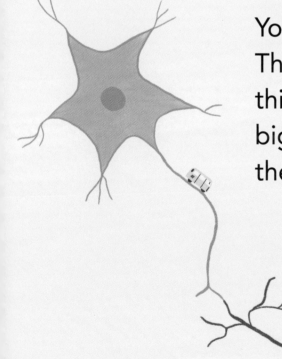

What is something you want to practice or learn? How will you practice, and how often?

Hard things make your brain grow.

Two kids are learning how to tie their shoes. One double-knots them in no time, and the other makes a mistake. Whose brain grew more?

Scientists researched this and found that your brain grows the most when you make a mistake. Struggling is good for your brain! Each challenge you face is an opportunity to grow stronger.

What are some positive things you can say to yourself when you make a mistake?

When your bus breaks down.

When you are doing something new and difficult, you may feel frustrated and overwhelmed. That's ok! Sharing how you feel with someone you trust can help.

In fact, there are lots of activities you can try to help yourself feel calm.

What is something that helps you feel better when you are upset? Here are a few ideas:

Take a walk

Listen to music

Squish slime

Blow bubbles

Ask for a hug

Color or draw

Drink water